The Biggest Dinosaurs

by Ruth Owen

Consultant:
Dougal Dixon, Paleontologist
Member of the Society of Vertebrate Paleontology
United Kingdom

BEARPORT
PUBLISHING

New York, New York

Credits

Cover, © James Kuether; 2–3, © Herschel Hoffmeyer/Shutterstock; 4–5, © James Kuether; 6–7, © James Kuether; 7T, © Wlad74/Shutterstock; 8–9, © Kenneth Lacovara; 10, Public Domain; 11, © James Kuether; 12–13 (L to R), © gan chonan/Shutterstock, © Yuri Schmidt/Shutterstock, © James Kuether, © doomu/Shutterstock, and © gualtiero boffi/Shutterstock; 14, © chrisstockphotography/Alamy; 14–15, © chrisstockphotography/Alamy; 15, © wk1003mike/Shutterstock; 16–17, © James Kuether; 16, © W. Scott McGill/Shutterstock; 17, © cjchiker/Shutterstock; 18, © Ryan M. Bolton/Shutterstock; 18–19, © The Washington Post/Getty Images; 20–21, © Herschel Hoffmeyer/Shutterstock; 22T, © Herschel Hoffmeyer/Shutterstock; 22B, © Yuri Photolife/Shutterstock; 23T, © Elnur/Shutterstock; 23B, © Andrey Shcherbukhin/Shutterstock.

Publisher: Kenn Goin
Senior Editor: Joyce Tavolacci
Creative Director: Spencer Brinker
Image Researcher: Ruth Owen Books

Library of Congress Cataloging-in-Publication Data

Names: Owen, Ruth, 1967– author.
Title: The biggest dinosaurs / by Ruth Owen.
Description: New York, New York : Bearport Publishing, [2019] | Series: The dino-sphere | Includes bibliographical references and index.
Identifiers: LCCN 2018049820 (print) | LCCN 2018053169 (ebook) | ISBN 9781642802542 (Ebook) | ISBN 9781642801859 (library)
Subjects: LCSH: Dinosaurs—Size—Juvenile literature.
Classification: LCC QE861.5 (ebook) | LCC QE861.5 .O8454 2019 (print) | DDC 567.9—dc23
LC record available at https://lccn.loc.gov/2018049820

For more information, write to Bearport Publishing Company, Inc., 45 West 21st Street, Suite 3B, New York, New York 10010. Printed in the United States of America.

10 9 8 7 6 5 4 3 2

Contents

Super Tall

Munch. Munch. Munch.

A huge dinosaur is eating leaves.

It towers above the trees.

It's a *Giraffatitan*, which means "giant giraffe."

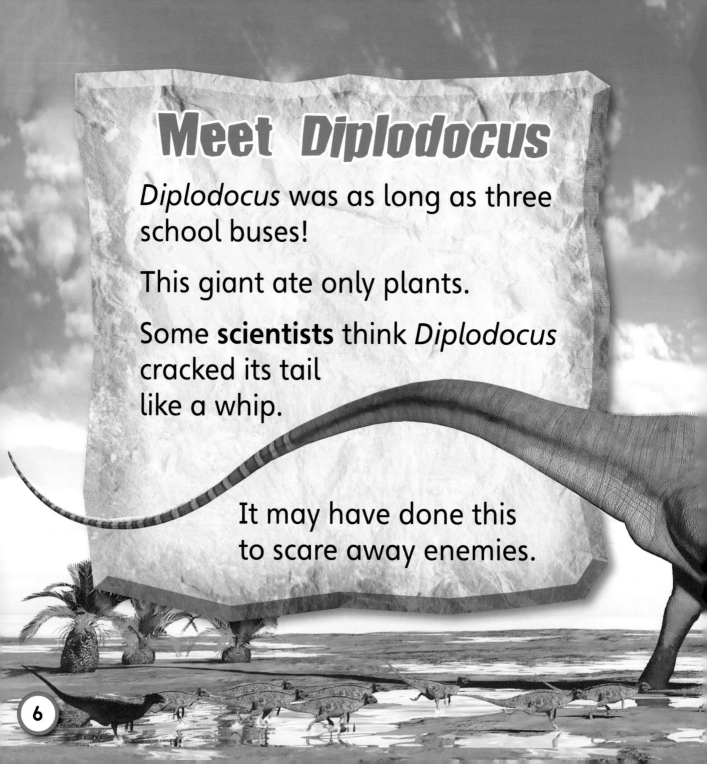

Meet Diplodocus

Diplodocus was as long as three school buses!

This giant ate only plants.

Some **scientists** think *Diplodocus* cracked its tail like a whip.

It may have done this to scare away enemies.

Every month,
a *Diplodocus's* teeth
fell out. Then new
teeth grew in!

Diplodocus
(dih-PLOD-uh-kuhs)

Giant Bones

How do we know that these huge dinosaurs existed?

Scientists have found their **fossils**!

In 2005, scientist Kenneth Lacovara found 145 huge fossils in Argentina.

dinosaur tail fossil

Kenneth Lacovara

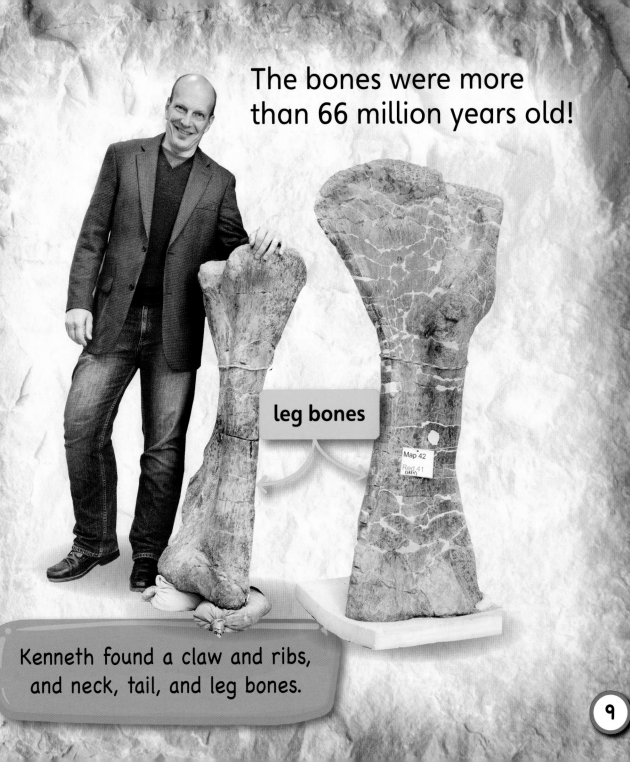

The bones were more than 66 million years old!

leg bones

Kenneth found a claw and ribs, and neck, tail, and leg bones.

A New Discovery

Kenneth fitted the fossil bones together like a jigsaw puzzle.

He had found a new kind of giant plant-eating dinosaur!

He named it *Dreadnoughtus*.

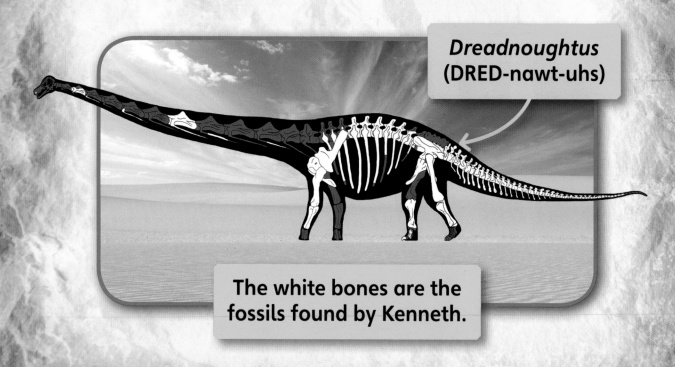

Dreadnoughtus (DRED-nawt-uhs)

The white bones are the fossils found by Kenneth.

The name *Dreadnoughtus* means "fears nothing."

Dreadnoughtus

Dreadnoughtus

How big was *Dreadnoughtus*?

It was 85 feet (26 m) long!

Its neck was longer than a school bus.

85 feet (26 m)

It weighed as much as 12 elephants!

Kenneth studied the bones of the *Dreadnoughtus*. He learned that the animal he found was young and still growing!

Rock Hard

In 2014, scientists dug up the bones of an even bigger dinosaur.

It was nearly as long as four school buses.

Its legs were as thick as tree trunks.

Named *Patagotitan*, it might be the biggest dinosaur that ever lived!

a scientist next to *Patagotitan*'s foot

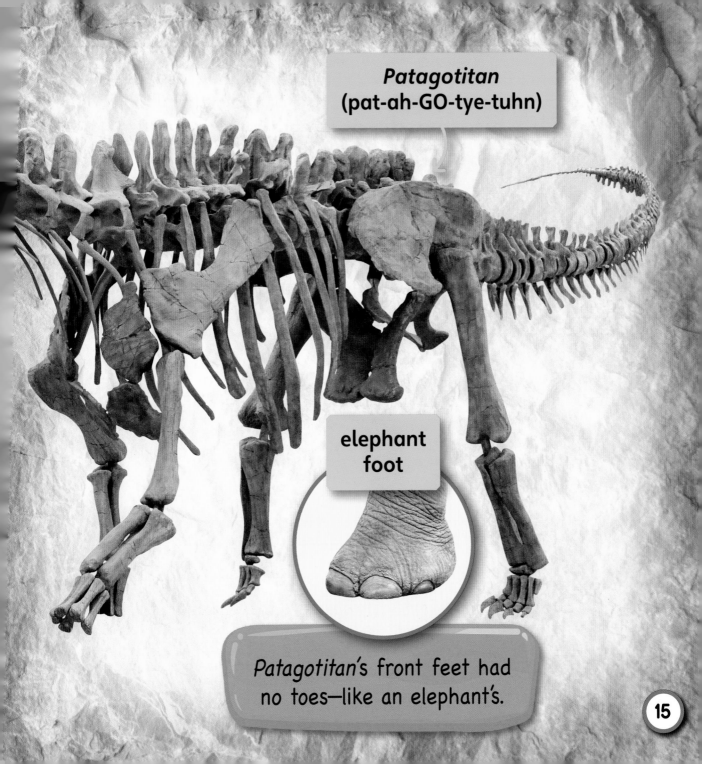

Patagotitan
(pat-ah-GO-tye-tuhn)

elephant foot

Patagotitan's front feet had no toes—like an elephant's.

Dinnertime!

The biggest dinosaurs were plant-eaters.

Scientists know this because they have found fossils of their poop!

poop fossil

Inside the poop are bits of grass, leaves, and twigs.

Futalognkosaurus
(FOO-tuh-lon-ko-sawr-uhs)

Plant-eating dinosaurs ate rocks to get enough **calcium**.

rocks from a dinosaur's stomach

Spiny Spinosaurus

Spinosaurus was longer than a school bus.

It had a long thin snout and teeth like a crocodile.

The dinosaur had **spines** on its back.

Its biggest spines were as tall as a person!

This *Spinosaurus* tooth is life-size.

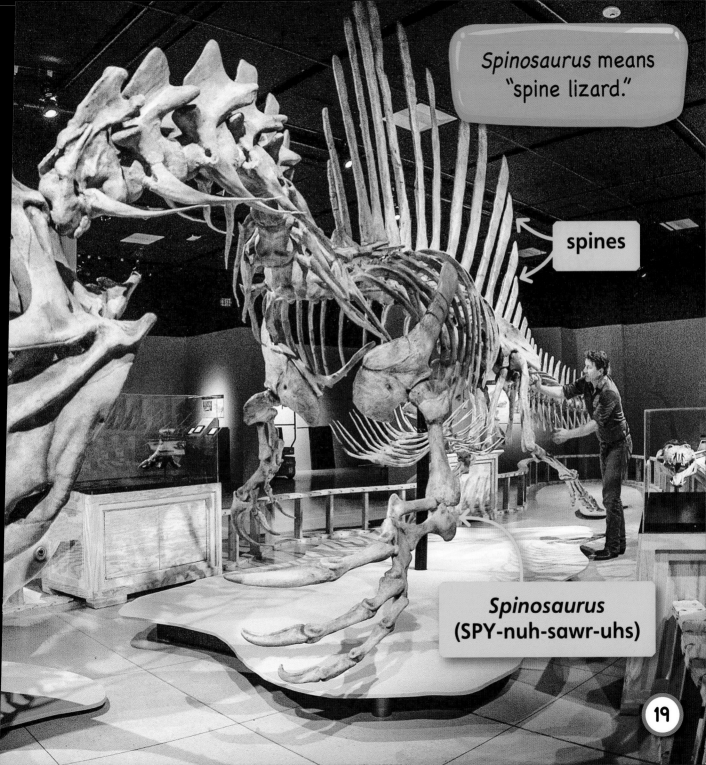

Spinosaurus means "spine lizard."

spines

Spinosaurus
(SPY-nuh-sawr-uhs)

Monster Meat-Eater

Scientists think that *Spinosaurus* could swim.

It probably lived in water and on land.

The giant hunter caught and ate big fish.

It's the longest meat-eating dinosaur found so far!

The spines on the dinosaur's back were covered with skin. They looked like a sail on a boat.

Glossary

calcium (KAL-see-uhm)
a substance needed
by animals for strong
bones and teeth

fossils (FOSS-uhlz)
the rocky remains of
animals and plants
that lived millions
of years ago

scientists
(SYE-uhn-tists)
people who
study nature
and the world

spines (SPYENZ)
hard, sharp
points on an
animal's body

Index

Read More

Lessem, Don. *Giant Plant-Eating Dinosaurs (Meet the Dinosaurs)*. Minneapolis, MN: Millbrook (2004).

Owen, Ruth. *Last Days of the Dinosaurs (The Dino-Sphere)*. New York: Bearport (2019).

Learn More Online

To learn more about dinosaurs, visit
www.bearportpublishing.com/dinosphere

About the Author

Ruth Owen has been developing and writing children's books for more than ten years. She first discovered dinosaurs when she was four years old—and loves them as much today as she did then!